My Heart Is Like a

ZOO

Michael Hall

GREENWILLOW BOOKS

An Imprint of HarperCollinsPublishers

My heart is like a zoo—

eager
as a
beaver,

steady
as a yak,

hopeful as a hungry heron
fishing for a snack . . .

silly
as a
seal,

rugged
as a
moose,

happy as a herd of hippos
drinking apple juice.

Snappy
as a
crab,

angry
as a
bear,

bothered as a bull
with a hornet in its hair.

Cool
as a
penguin,

quiet as a caterpillar
wearing knitted socks.

Frightened
as a
rabbit,

jumpy
as a
frog,

gloomy as a lone coyote
walking in the fog.

Brave
as a
lion,

thoughtful
as an
owl,

peaceful as a portly walrus
lounging on a towel.

Cozy
as a
clam,

chatty

as a

jay,

tired as a
zookeeper
who's had
a busy day.

For
Alice

My Heart Is Like a Zoo

Copyright © 2010 by Michael Hall

All rights reserved. Printed in the U.S.A.
For information address
HarperCollins Children's Books,
a division of HarperCollins Publishers,
10 East 53rd Street, New York, NY 10022.
www.harpercollinschildrens.com

Digital art was used
to prepare the full-color art.

The text type is 30-point
Avenir 65 Medium.

Library of Congress Cataloging-in-Publication Data
Hall, Michael, (date).
My heart is like a zoo / by Michael Hall.
 p. cm.
"Greenwillow Books."
Summary: Depicts in rhyming text how love can be many
different things, such as eager as a beaver, steady as a yak,
or silly as a seal.
ISBN 978-0-06-191510-9 (trade bdg.)
ISBN 978-0-06-191511-6 (lib. bdg.)
[1. Stories in rhyme. 2. Love—Fiction.
3. Zoo animals—Fiction.] I. Title.
PZ8.3.H1483My 2010   [E]—dc22   2009017818

10 11 12 13 CG/WOR First Edition 10 9 8 7 6 5 4 3 2

Greenwillow Books